KU-594-413

LITTLE TIGER PRESS LTD,
an imprint of the Little Tiger Group
1 Coda Studios, 189 Munster Road,
London SW6 6AW
www.littletiger.co.uk

First published in Great Britain 2015
This edition published 2019
Text by Amelia Hepworth
Text copyright © Little Tiger Press Ltd 2015
Illustrations copyright © Tim Warnes 2010, 2015
Visit Tim Warnes at www.timwarnes.com
Tim Warnes has asserted his right to be identified as the illustrator
of this work under the Copyright, Designs and Patents Act, 1988
A CIP catalogue record for this book is available from the British Library

All rights reserved · ISBN: 978-1-78881-458-4
Printed in China · LTP/1800/3482/0820
4 6 8 10 9 7 5 3

This Little Tiger book belongs to:

_____

_____

_____

I Love You to the MOON and BACK

TIM WARNES

LITTLE TIGER
LONDON

I love our time
together as we start
each happy day.

I love our bathtime silliness –
the way we splash
and play!

I love to lift you way up high,
so you feel really tall!

We'll climb the highest
mountain-tops –

hold tight and you
won't fall.

I love to share the
magic of the shining
skies above,

And think of all
the different ways that
we can show our love ...

Like when we're
touching noses,

Playing chase,

Or seeing friends,

Our love is always
with us, and it never,
ever ends.

So snuggle safely
in my arms;
our day is
nearly done.

I love you to the moon and stars, my precious little one.